THE SECRET EXPLORERS®
AND THE PLANT POACHERS

CONTENTS

1 A woodland wonder   4

2 Flytraps in danger   20

3 Poachers!   36

4 A chase in the dark   48

5 Tracking and trailing   62

6 Calling for help   74

7 The trap is set   88

8 Flytrap rescue   *102*

The Venus flytrap   *116*

Other carnivorous plants   *118*

Carolina wildlife   *120*

Quiz   *122*

Glossary   *124*

Acknowledgements   *128*

Chapter One
A WOODLAND WONDER

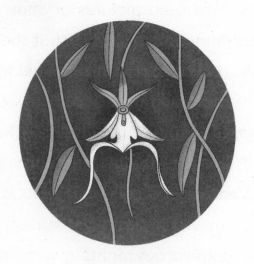

"No WAY!" Leah gasped. She couldn't believe her eyes. This was like finding a fairy at the bottom of your garden, only better.

She leaned her bike gently against a beech tree. As she walked across the woodland clearing, she kept her gaze fixed on the tiny plant she'd spotted. The closer she got, the more excited she became. She was looking at a ghost orchid!

Leah had seen pictures of ghost orchids on the internet and in books, but she'd never thought she would ever see a real one. And she'd definitely never thought she would see one growing so close to her home in Oxfordshire, in the south of England. Ghost orchids were incredibly rare and endangered. In fact, they were so hard to find in her country that people had thought they were extinct.

She would have to keep the plant's location a secret, so it didn't get dug up and stolen. Leah didn't mind. After all, she already had another big secret, which none of her friends or family even suspected...

She knelt down next to the ghost orchid. It was white and delicate. *No wonder it's called a ghost orchid*, she thought. Unlike so many other plants, it had no green in it.

Leah was an expert on plants, so she knew what that meant. Green plants contained chlorophyll, the substance that turned sunlight into the energy they needed to grow. But the little ghost orchid got its energy in quite a different way. It sucked up nutrition from the rotting vegetation

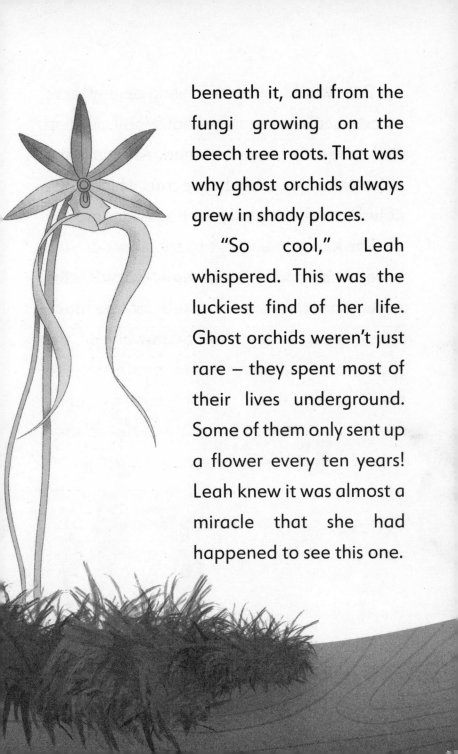

beneath it, and from the fungi growing on the beech tree roots. That was why ghost orchids always grew in shady places.

"So cool," Leah whispered. This was the luckiest find of her life. Ghost orchids weren't just rare – they spent most of their lives underground. Some of them only sent up a flower every ten years! Leah knew it was almost a miracle that she had happened to see this one.

But it was time to check on her own plants. Leah had a greenhouse full of them at home, and they all needed care and attention. She cycled home as fast as she could, still feeling excited about finding the ghost orchid.

She skidded to a halt outside the greenhouse. As she reached for the door, she stopped in her tracks. Glowing on the glass was a compass symbol.

"Yes!" she cheered.

Leah had a badge just like that on her jacket. It stood for the Secret Explorers, the group of problem-solving experts she belonged to. Now Leah felt even more excited. The Secret Explorers were being called for a new mission!

Leah opened the door and walked through. Instead of the familiar greenhouse with its rows of exotic plants, she entered a strange tunnel of blinding white light. Wind roared around her...

...and in the next second, she was back in the Exploration Station!

"Leah, here!" she called, and gave a salute, like she always did when she arrived.

The Exploration Station was an amazing hidden base, with walls of polished black stone, displays of objects the Explorers had brought back from their missions, and huge comfortable chairs and sofas for relaxing on. A row of computer workstations stood to one side, so the Explorers who weren't chosen to go on the missions could still offer help.

Leah headed for the big sofa to wait for the others. She passed by the huge map of the world on the floor, on which dots would light up to show them where their missions were. Above the map, an image of the Milky Way glittered on the domed ceiling.

One by one, the other Explorers arrived through the glowing door and joined Leah in the lounge area.

"Ollie here!" shouted a boy with boots all muddy from trekking through the rainforest.

"Kiki here!" called the Engineering Explorer.

"Roshni here," called the Space Explorer. She glanced at Ollie's muddy footprints, Kiki's fingers and Leah's dirty knees. "Wow, the Exploration Station is messy today!"

Cheng came running in, wiping dust on his T-shirt. "Cheng here!" Leah guessed he'd been breaking rocks open with his geologist's hammer.

Tamiko, the Dinosaur Explorer, and Connor, the Marine Explorer, were next to arrive. Last came Gustavo, the History Explorer, with cobwebs in his hair. "Been up in the attic looking through old books," he explained as he brushed them off.

"Any guesses what the mission's about?" said Kiki.

"Maybe the astronauts on the International Space Station need rescuing!" said Roshni.

"Or a submarine might be in trouble," suggested Connor.

Just then, a light appeared on the map on the floor.

"That's North Carolina," Cheng said. "It's on the east coast of the USA."

A shaft of light projected up from the dot, with a screen at the top. The screen showed a small green plant growing from the forest floor. It had petals with spikes at the edges, like teeth inside a set of jaws.

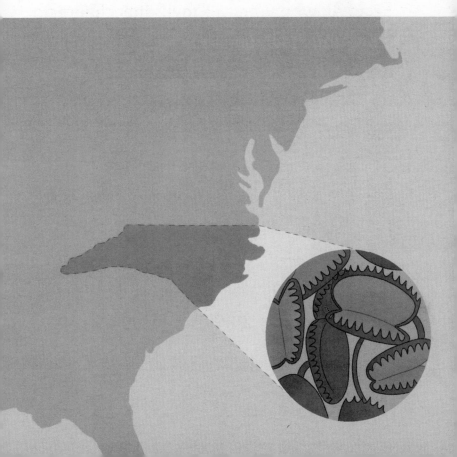

Leah recognised the plant instantly. "A Venus flytrap! The mission must be something to do with them." She crossed the fingers of both hands for luck, and wished super-hard that she would be chosen.

Ping! Her compass badge lit up.

"Yay!" she cheered, leaping up from her seat. "I get to go!"

"Good call, Exploration Station," said Roshni, and everyone agreed. Leah knew more about plants than any of them. Then Gustavo's badge lit up too.

"Awesome!" he said. "Looks like I'm coming with you, Leah."

"Welcome on board, History Explorer!" Leah said. She gave him a thumbs-up and they grinned at one another.

"I wonder what history has got to do with Venus flytraps?" said Roshni.

"I dunno," Kiki said, "but the Exploration Station always choses the right Explorers for every mission, doesn't it?" She walked over to a control console. "You two ready? Let's get you on your way!"

She pulled a lever and a platform rose up from the floor. In the middle was a vehicle named the Beagle, after Charles Darwin's ship. He'd been a famous scientist and explorer. Leah always giggled when she saw it rising up so grandly, because it looked like an old go-kart, with wonky wheels and flaking paint. However, like all of them, it had secrets too.

Leah and Gustavo climbed on board. They strapped themselves in. A large red button on the dashboard read "START". Once that button was pressed, there was no going back.

Leah held her breath – and shoved the button down.

They shot forwards, much faster than should have been possible. Blazing, brilliant light shone all around them. The Beagle shuddered violently as if it were falling to bits, but Leah knew it was just the transformation starting.

As they zoomed faster and faster through the light, the Beagle changed its form. A metal frame rose up around them, and the little steering wheel became large and sturdy in Gustavo's hands...

The light faded away. The Beagle was chugging along on big, chunky wheels instead of little wonky ones. Leah felt humid air on her face. Tall trees rose up around them. A clean, salty smell was in her nostrils. They must be close to the sea.

In a blur of colour, a hummingbird whizzed past Leah, making her jump.

"Wow!" she gasped.

Gustavo glanced around. "I guess we made it to North Carolina," he said with a grin. "And just look what the Beagle's turned into."

Leah looked down, and realised she was now at the wheel of a huge, rugged, two-seater quad bike!

"Oh, wow," she said. "Just when I thought this mission couldn't get any cooler!"

Chapter Two
FLYTRAPS IN DANGER

"So what do you think our mission is?" Gustavo asked.

"Let's check out our equipment," Leah suggested. "That might give us an idea."

She brought the Beagle to a stop. The Beagle made a helpful **BEEP**, and an arrow lit up on the dashboard, pointing backwards.

Leah and Gustavo climbed out and

headed round to the back, where a compartment opened with a happy **BING!** sound from the Beagle.

"Thanks, buddy!" Leah said.

They looked through the gear the Exploration Station had provided. "We've got water bottles, food, sun cream, a first-aid kit, and insect repellent," Leah said.

Gustavo lifted out a large tablet with a compass logo on the back. "Look at all the apps on this!" he said. "HD camera, GPS, and communications so we can stay in touch with the others. But what's there at the back?"

Leah peered in. "A tent and some sleeping bags."

"Cool," Gustavo said. "I can't quite figure it out, though. How can we help the Venus flytraps by going camping?"

Leah shrugged. "Only one way to find out. Let's explore!"

She started to go, but Gustavo stopped her. "Wait. We shouldn't leave the Beagle sitting out here for anyone to find."

"But how are we meant to hide it?" asked Leah.

Gustavo thought for a moment. "In World War Two, they hid tanks in foliage so they wouldn't be spotted. We could do the same."

"Thanks, History Explorer!" Leah said with a laugh.

It didn't take Leah long to find a group of tall bushes, thick with leaves. They parked the Beagle deep inside and moved the branches around to hide it. Taking only the tablet and the first-aid supplies with them for now, they set off.

High above them, white birds with long yellowish beaks were passing by. "Pelicans!" Leah explained. "That means the sea must be close, so we're in a coastal forest. There should be lots of amazing wildlife to spot."

Sure enough, a little grey shape soon went sailing past overhead, gliding from one tree to another with its arms and legs spread out. It had flaps of skin between its limbs that looked like wings.

"Cool! What was that?" asked Gustavo.

"A flying squirrel," Leah replied. "They don't actually fly, though. They glide, using their skin flaps like parachutes."

They crossed a weathered old bridge over a river. A catfish briefly swam up from the depths. Leah pointed out the long whisker-like features by its mouth, which gave the fish its name. Then, just as Leah was thinking about stopping for a water break, she spotted some little green plants growing up from the soil. Plants that looked as if they had tiny fanged mouths...

"There they are!" she yelled, and they hurried over.

"Are those the Venus flytraps?" Gustavo said. He kneeled down to peer at the hinged, open leaves with their long tooth-like spines. "I thought they'd be bigger."

Leah laughed. "They aren't man-eating monster plants from outer space! They only grow to ten centimetres tall. But they are carnivorous. That means they eat meat."

"Amazing!" said Gustavo. "But they don't look like they need our help. I wonder what our mission could be?"

Leah grabbed his arm. "Whoa, watch this! It's dinnertime!"

An ant had just crawled inside one of the open leafy heads. Leah and Gustavo watched in fascination. The ant moved ever so slightly... and the trap snapped shut. The spines meshed together like long fingers, closing the ant inside.

"Wow!" Gustavo said. "How did it know the ant was there?"

Leah showed him one of the plant heads that was still open. "See those tiny hairs on the inside? They're trigger hairs," she explained. "Touch one, and the trap gets ready to close. But unless one of the hairs is touched in the next twenty seconds, the trap will stay open."

Gustavo gasped. "You're saying these little plants can count?"

Leah grinned. "The trigger hairs have to work like that, or else the trap would close every time something landed on it – even if it's just a raindrop or a leaf," she said. "This way, the plant can be sure that it's trapping an insect, because only an insect would move around and touch the hairs like that. It means the plant doesn't waste energy trapping things it can't eat."

Gustavo peered at the closed trap. "What happens to the ant now?"

"It gets digested," Leah said brightly. "There are juices in there, a bit like the inside of a stomach."

Gustavo got up and dusted himself down. "You know... I've seen creatures eat plants loads of times. But I've never seen a plant eat a creature!"

They started walking on through the forest. "Flytraps evolved that way," Leah said. "They kind of had to, really. They couldn't get enough nutrients from the soil here, so they had to start eating insects." She thought of the ghost orchid back home, having to feed on fungi and rotting vegetation. It was a similar story.

"Hey, look at that!" Gustavo pointed through the trees.

Ahead stood a building made of wood with lots of big glass windows. A sign read: **"NORTH CAROLINA CONSERVATION GROUP AND SEED BANK."**

"Maybe we could find out about our mission in there," said Gustavo.

Leah nodded. "It's a conservation centre, so they'll want to help the plants!" she exclaimed. "Let's ask."

NORTH CAROLINA CONSERVATION GROUP AND SEED BANK

They headed in through the open door. The whole place smelled like a hothouse, and reminded Leah of trips to the local garden centre with her family. The inside was like a laboratory, with workbenches and trays of soil filled with seedlings. Groups of people were tending to the plants, spraying them with water and carefully repotting them.

Leah noticed that one woman was examining a Venus flytrap. She went up to her, with Gustavo following. "Excuse me?" said Leah. "Is that plant okay? Can we help at all?"

The woman looked over the rim of her glasses at her, and smiled. "I hope so! I'm Luisa, and I'm a botanist. You know what that is?"

"A plant scientist," said Leah immediately.

Luisa smiled even more. "Here at the centre, we botanists are looking after some Venus flytraps that have been rescued from poachers."

"Poachers?" Leah and Gustavo said together, in amazement.

"They steal the flytraps from the wild and sell them," Luisa explained. "It's a terrible problem. One of the only places in the world where Venus flytraps grow in the wild is here in North Carolina. These plants are having a hard enough time as it is, as their habitat is being destroyed by people cutting down the trees." Luisa gave a sad sigh. "Poaching is making the problem even worse. Venus flytraps are now an endangered species."

Leah and Gustavo looked at each other. "That's awful!" Gustavo said.

"Let me show you something," said Luisa. She handed Leah and Gustavo a thin glass rod each. "Give the inside of the plant's heads a little poke, to test its reaction. But be gentle."

They each touched their rods to the trigger hairs inside the flower head. But this flytrap didn't snap shut like the one they'd seen in the forest. It closed slowly, as if it was worn out.

Luisa sighed. "That's a bad sign. Poachers don't look after the plants they steal. This poor flytrap is pretty run down."

"Can you do anything?" said Leah, feeling very sorry for it.

"We'll nurse it back to health, don't worry," said Luisa. "Then we'll replant it in the wild. This one was lucky – there are plenty more we can't get to in time."

Gustavo whispered to Leah, "I think I just figured out what our mission is."

"Me too," said Leah. "We need to protect the Venus flytraps from those rotten poachers!"

Chapter Three
POACHERS!

The Exploration Station could do many amazing things, but one of the most useful was the way it could send the Secret Explorers back to the exact moment they left home to go on their missions. This meant that even if a mission took many hours, the Explorers' families wouldn't get worried that they hadn't come back.

Just as well, thought Leah, as she looked up at the stars twinkling in the North Carolina sky.

At dusk, she and Gustavo had pitched the tent next to a large patch of flytraps and settled in for a long night watching over them. Now it was the very darkest hour of the night, just before the dawn.

At least they weren't hungry. The Beagle's cool box had supplied sandwiches and drinks, and they'd munched them outside the tent. Now there was nothing to do but sit, and watch, and wait...

Leah felt alert and excited. The forest after dark was full of strange noises as the nocturnal animals went about their lives. As the Biology Explorer, it was a thrill for Leah to be here and listen to them. Gustavo, on the other hand, was clearly a little creeped out.

He froze as something swooped past, a quick blur of shadow even darker than the surrounding forest. "What was that?" he hissed.

"It's just a bat," Leah reassured him. "It's out hunting."

From somewhere close by came a deep croaking noise, and then another. Gustavo leapt to his feet. "And what are those?! Are they coming this way?"

Leah tried not to laugh. "Don't worry, they're just frogs. They're croaking at each other to say, 'this is my territory, stay away!'"

Gustavo sat down again, and seemed to relax a bit. "Thanks. I guess the night's less scary when you know about biology."

Later on, he even grinned when he heard a distant hooting. "That's an owl, right?"

"A great horned owl, by the sound of it," said Leah. "Ooh, listen! Two bobcats are fighting!"

They sat for a moment and listened to the hoarse, throaty yowls the bobcats made.

"This is amazing," Gustavo said happily.

"I know," Leah replied. "I wish we could stay here all w—"

Cough.

They both fell silent instantly. *That was no animal*, Leah thought. *That was a human being!* Her arms broke out in goosebumps.

The cough came again. It was close. Very close.

Leah and Gustavo kept very still, listening hard. Leah wanted to climb inside the tent, zip the flap shut and pull the sleeping bag over her head.

Nearby, someone was talking. The words were too faint to hear clearly, but Leah knew one thing now for sure. They weren't alone in the dark forest.

"Poachers?" Gustavo whispered.

"Only one way to find out," Leah whispered back.

"Investigate?"

"Yeah? We should take something to record them with, just in case."

Leah grabbed the tablet with the built-in camera from the tent. She and Gustavo set off through the forest, closing in on the spot where the voices were coming from.

Tree trunks loomed out of the darkness. Branches dangled in their path, and they had to duck and dodge around them. Thick mud squelched underfoot.

"Still with me?" Leah whispered.

"Yeah," came Gustavo's voice from close by.

He sounded just as frightened as Leah felt.

Through the trees Leah saw a light up ahead, bobbing and unsteady. A flashlight! The pair of them hunkered down and crept slowly forward, until they reached the edge of a clearing.

A man and a woman were crouched down. The man held the flashlight, shining it so the woman could see what she was doing. She held a shovel. Next to her was a box.

As Leah watched, she saw the woman sink the shovel into the earth and lift up a Venus flytrap. She tipped it into the box and went back for another.

"Keep that light steady!" the woman hissed angrily. "I nearly cut through a plant, you idiot. These things are worth money!"

Freezing water seemed to run through Leah's veins.

"They're definitely poachers!" she whispered.

"We've got to stop them," Gustavo said. "Can you video them, and catch them in the act?"

Summoning all her bravery, Leah edged forwards until she could almost reach out and grab the man's coat.

With shaking hands she lifted the tablet, pointed it at the poachers and pressed the record button. There wasn't much light, but it should be enough. *Oh, please*, she thought, *let this work...*

The woman grunted as she worked the spade. Earth rattled as plant after plant fell into the box. Leah kept the camera as steady as she could.

And then the darkness seemed to come alive. With a grunt, something gigantic rose up to her left and shook the undergrowth. Leah couldn't see what it was, but it was definitely some kind of animal. A big one. And it was so close she could hear it breathing!

The poachers heard the sound of cracking branches and swishing ferns too. They leapt to their feet.

"Someone's here!" the woman said. She snatched up the box full of flytraps. "Let's go!"

And before Leah's horrified eyes, the poachers went sprinting off through the trees, leaving her in pitch darkness – with an enormous animal...

Chapter Four
A CHASE IN THE DARK

Leah could still see the poachers' flashlight, winking in and out through the trees. She grabbed Gustavo by the arm. "Come on!"

They had to catch the poachers – and they had to get away from the huge animal lurking in the trees!

The two Explorers sprinted through the dark forest. Every twist and turn brought them new danger, as roots threatened to trip them and thorns ripped at their clothes. From up ahead came a yell as one of the poachers blundered through a low-hanging branch.

Suddenly, the poachers' light vanished. They'd lost them! Gasping, Leah peered into the night. She saw nothing but swaying branches and the darkness of the forest.

Then Gustavo yelled, "This way!" He pulled her around, back to where the flashlight was now glimmering. The poachers had doubled back on themselves.

Clever, Leah thought. *They must be trying to outfox us!*

She set off after them, grateful for Gustavo's quick thinking. But without warning, the light vanished again.

Leah stumbled forward a few steps, until the truth dawned on her. The light hadn't disappeared because the poachers had changed course. Something was blotting it out. A large, dark shape loomed up in front of them. A snuffling, grunting sound reached her ears.

It was the animal they'd disturbed earlier! And Leah had realised what it was...

She grabbed Gustavo and held on for dear life. "Stop!" she hissed at him.

"Why? What..."

"It's a black bear!"

The moon came out from behind a cloud and she saw the bear clearly for the first time. It was standing upright, at least six feet tall, its hulking body covered all over with jet-black fur. They had almost run right into it.

To her relief, the bear wasn't attacking. It dropped down on to all fours and grubbed about in the undergrowth, making huffing noises.

Gustavo swallowed hard. "Is it going to eat us?"

"Probably not," Leah said. "If it was a grizzly bear, we'd be in big trouble. Black bears aren't as aggressive."

"Oh man, am I glad you said that!" Gustavo sighed with relief.

"We've still got to be very careful, though," Leah warned. "We're in the bear's territory, and we weren't invited. Those poachers must have disturbed it. No wonder it's in a bad mood."

"So what do we do?"

"We skirt around it," Leah said.

They edged through the forest, giving

the bear a very wide berth. Meanwhile, the poachers' flashlight dwindled off into the distance like a teasing will-o-the-wisp. By the time Leah and Gustavo had made their way past the grumpy bear, the flashlight had completely vanished.

Leah groaned. "They've gone! And so have the stolen Venus flytraps. I don't know how we're going to get them back now," she said sadly.

"We'll think of something," said Gustavo. He pointed to where the eastern sky was changing from black to blue-grey. "Look, the sun's coming up. I know what we ought to do next."

"What?"

"Eat breakfast," Gustavo said. "An army marches on its stomach, after all. Napoleon said that."

Back at their tents, Gustavo prepared a hasty breakfast of cereal bars and fruit juice. Leah sat munching, with the tablet on her knees. She could imagine the poachers laughing, driving through the night with their stolen plants. They'd gotten away with it!

"We've got to save those flytraps," she said. "But how?"

Gustavo said, "You filmed the poachers in the act, didn't you? Let's examine the footage."

Leah pressed "PLAY" and the pair of them settled back to watch the video. But her heart sank. Instead of the crystal-clear evidence she had expected, there was nothing but blurry trees.

Then came an image of Gustavo's leg, and a lot of bear noises, followed by a wobbly sequence as they ran through the forest. You could hardly see the poachers at all, much less their faces.

"So much for my photography skills!" Leah said with dismay. "What are we going to do now?"

Gustavo frowned thoughtfully. "Well," he said, "we historians gather evidence and use it to build up a picture of what happened in the past. If we can find some evidence, maybe we can get an idea where the poachers took the flytraps."

"Brilliant!" Leah cheered.

Gustavo grinned, and the two of them raced off, trying to find their way back to the spot where the poachers had been.

They had only run a little way when Gustavo suddenly skidded to a halt. "Woah!"

"What is it?" Leah couldn't see anything up ahead.

Gustavo rubbed his eyes and pointed to a group of little brownish-grey rocks down on the forest floor. "Either I'm going crazy, or those rocks just moved!"

Leah went in for a closer look. The rocks were definitely moving.

Then, under the edges of the rocks, she saw eyes, little snouts, and clawed toes. The upper parts were banded, armoured shells. Suddenly, she understood what she was looking at.

"Gustavo, these aren't rocks at all," she cried out. "They're four baby armadillos!"

Leah watched the little armadillos crawling around at her feet. They were adorable, but she knew they ought to be left alone. Their mother would look after them properly.

Wait a moment – where was their mother?

She looked around, parting the nearby undergrowth as she searched for a bigger armadillo. But no matter how hard she looked, she couldn't find the mother. There weren't even any tracks.

"Come on, Leah!" Gustavo called from a way back down the trail. "We need to track down those poachers!"

Leah felt torn in two. On the one hand, Gustavo was right – they had to find the poachers and save the Venus flytraps. But on the other hand...

The Secret Explorers never abandon anyone who needs help, she thought. She knew what they had to do.

"We'll find those poachers," she called to Gustavo. "But these babies have lost their mother, and we need to find her first. And fast!"

Chapter Five
TRACKING AND TRAILING

They searched through the undergrowth for the mother armadillo, peering under clumps of ferns and around bushes.

"I wonder how the babies lost their mother," Gustavo said, lifting a fern to check underneath.

"Maybe something scared them and they ran away," Leah guessed.

"I bet it was the poachers," said Gustavo grimly. "Hey do you think the mother armadillo can tell her babies apart? They all look exactly the same to me!"

Leah said, "Actually, they are exactly the same. Right down to their genes."

Gustavo stared. "Like identical twins?"

"Bingo!" said Leah. "Armadillos almost always have four identical babies. They're the only mammal that does."

After a while, Gustavo called Leah over to see a little tunnel dug into the earth. It was about twenty centimetres wide.

"That's got to be the armadillo burrow," she said. "Hopefully, the mother is still inside! We need to figure out a way to lead her to the babies."

"Maybe we could make a trail of fruit?" Gustavo suggested.

"Great idea," said Leah, "except armadillos are mostly insectivores. That means they eat insects. Just like Venus flytraps!"

Leah directed Gustavo to look for rotten branches on the ground. Those were much more likely to have insects and grubs living inside them. Gustavo almost tripped over a whole rotten tree trunk covered in moss and vines. Leah peeled back a length of its spongy bark to reveal hundreds of scuttling bugs underneath.

Gustavo immediately scooped them up in his cupped hands. Leah could tell he didn't like it very much, but he was putting up with it for the armadillos' sake. She held out her own hands and he tipped some of the creepy-crawlies into them.

Soon they had made a bug trail between the baby armadillos and the burrow. They hid behind some bushes to watch and wait, keeping very still and making as little noise as possible.

Gustavo suddenly frowned. "Leah, did you walk over that way at all?" He pointed at a patch of crushed vegetation.

"No, why?" Leah asked.

"Could it be an armadillo trail?" Gustavo wondered. "Maybe we've got it wrong, and the mother went off in that direction."

Leah shook her head. "It's too big for an armadillo," she said. "It's all trampled down, like a person ran through it..." She gasped. "Gustavo, I think you've found evidence the poachers came this—oh, look!"

A fully grown armadillo was nosing her way out of the burrow. Leah and Gustavo grinned at one another. It was the mother! But would she notice the bug trail?

The mother armadillo sniffed all around her – and gobbled up one of the bugs.

"It's working!" Gustavo whispered.

"I hope she finds her babies soon," Leah whispered back. "We've got a trail of our own to follow!"

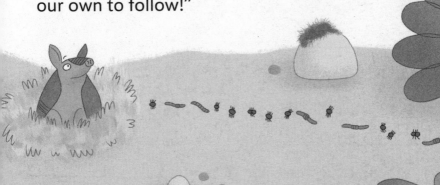

To her relief, the armadillo began trotting up the bug trail. When she got close to where her babies were huddled, they scurried to meet her, squeaking excitedly.

Leah and Gustavo watched for a while as the reunited armadillo family snuffled around one another, before the babies followed their mother back towards the burrow.

"Thank goodness they're safe!" Gustavo said.

"Good job!" said Leah, giving him a high-five. "Now let's check out that evidence..."

They headed over to where Gustavo had noticed the crushed grass. There was definitely a faint trail here. They bent over the squashed leaves and studied them carefully.

"I can't tell much from this," Leah admitted. "How about you?"

"Not by itself, but look!" Gustavo ran over to a second spot. "The grass is flattened in this direction, see? So the poachers must have run from there through here."

Leah nodded. "That makes sense. Let's follow the trail!"

It led over a grassy area, then past a thick cluster of trees. With a start, Leah noticed a small patch of flytraps next to a lot of freshly dug holes. "They must have helped themselves to some more flytraps on the way!" she said.

"I guess they felt safe enough to steal more, once they'd shaken us off last night," Gustavo said.

"Those poachers must have taken hundreds of plants," Leah said gloomily. "Oh, I wish we'd been able to stop them!"

"There's still a chance," Gustavo said encouragingly. "If they hadn't been so greedy and dug up more plants, we wouldn't know for sure it was them who made this trail, would we? Now we know for certain that they were here, so we can try to find where they went!"

Leah nodded. She was glad Gustavo was on the mission. His positive attitude cheered her up, too.

They headed further along the path, following the crushed grass towards a little stream.

I'm hot on your trail, poachers, Leah thought. *I'll get you yet!*

Chapter Six
CALLING FOR HELP

"Aha!" said Gustavo. Leah was standing beside him on the bank of the stream. He pointed out some thin branches on the other side of the water. "See where those branches are snapped? Now put the scene together in your mind."

Leah tried to picture the poachers moving through the night. "It was dark, so they wouldn't have been able to see any stepping stones... So they would have had to take a blind leap... So they probably didn't see those branches at all! They just crashed through them and kept going."

"Good work!" Gustavo jumped over the stream, just as the poachers would have done. Leah followed, full of the thrill of the chase. She couldn't wait for Gustavo to spot the next clue.

But it was Leah who saw a faint impression in the mud. "Gustavo, hold up! Isn't that a footprint?"

Gustavo looked down at the U-shaped imprint in the ground. "Definitely. Good spot."

"It looks a bit weird," Leah said. "Like it's only the front half of the foot."

"It is," Gustavo explained. "Because when you run, you don't bring your foot down flat, do you? Only the front part comes into contact with the ground."

"The poachers were running. It must have been them," Leah said.

Gustavo pondered. "Well, it's a good job you spotted this print, because it means they suddenly swerved off this way, through these bushes. I wonder why?"

"Bear tracks!" Leah said, pointing at the ground. "I guess the black bear from last night has a mate."

Gustavo grinned. "You'd make a brilliant historian!"

There was a lot more leaf cover overhead, which meant a lot less sunlight reaching the forest floor, which meant less bracken and more patches of bare earth. They found the footprint trail with ease. Leah noticed the prints were more regular, meaning the poachers had slowed down. Then Gustavo pointed out something shiny and picked it up.

"A chocolate wrapper," he said. "If they had time for a snack, they weren't in a hurry anymore. So they must have thought they were safe."

Leah pocketed it, making a disgusted face.

They searched the ground for more footprints, but neither of them could find any.

Leah felt frustrated. "What if there aren't any more prints to find?" she muttered. "If the trail's gone cold, then we're out of luck..."

"Let's check over there, where the wrapper was," Gustavo suggested. "I've got a hunch that it might have fallen out of something...or been thrown out."

Leah pushed through some ferns and gave a shout. "Tyre marks! So that's how they got away!"

"I knew it!" cried Gustavo. "They ate the chocolate bar in their vehicle and threw the wrapper out of the window."

Leah scowled. "These poachers are the worst – they're litterbugs, too!"

Gustavo looked at the tyre tracks snaking off through the forest. "They could be anywhere by now."

Leah felt new determination fill her. "Then let's get the Beagle and follow them."

Moments later, they were racing along through the forest with Leah at the wheel. The engine roared and the Beagle made excited *BEEPS* as they went.

It was a long drive, but eventually the tyre marks ended at the edge of the forest, right by a road. They had only gone a little way along it when Leah caught sight of a row of large buildings up ahead. She parked the Beagle and she and Gustavo went for a closer look.

"What do you think they are?" Gustavo wondered.

Leah looked at their high walls, metal roofs and small windows. "Warehouses, I think."

They edged closer, listening carefully in case anyone drove up. Soon they could see into the warehouse parking lots. There were lots of cars and trucks parked outside.

"The flytraps have to be inside one of these warehouses," said Gustavo. "But which one? We can't search all of them."

"If only we knew what the poachers' vehicle looked like – then we could find the right warehouse," Leah said.

Gustavo's eyes widened. "That gives me an idea!" he said. "We've done as much as we can by ourselves. I think it's time to call in the Secret Explorers!"

He reached into his backpack and pulled out the tablet they'd found in the Beagle. "Gustavo and Leah calling the Exploration Station. Requesting assistance!"

After a tense moment Leah saw their friends appear, sitting at their computer desks.

"Exploration Station, standing by!" said Roshni. "How can we help?"

Leah quickly explained what their mission was, and how the poachers were almost within their grasp. "We just need to find out which of those vehicles belongs to them!" she finished.

"And I have an idea how." Gustavo went back to the edge of the forest and held the screen so that it showed the tyre tracks. "Can you run this through the computers and see what they come up with?"

"On it!" said Kiki.

The Secret Explorers turned to their computers and got to work, while Leah and Gustavo nervously watched the road. If the poachers drove off with stolen plants now, there would be no way to stop them.

"Bingo!" yelled Ollie after a few minutes. "We have a match!"

"Go ahead, Ollie," Leah said excitedly.

Ollie said, "They're special tyres with extra deep tread. Only two sorts of vehicle use them. An ATV called a Ranger 268, or a truck called a Viper Strike."

Leah and Gustavo high-fived one another. "Thanks for the help, guys!" Leah told the Secret Explorers.

"No worries," Ollie said.

All the other Explorers chimed in. "Good luck!" They waved goodbye and Gustavo turned off the screen.

Leah and Gustavo climbed back into the Beagle. They drove it as close to the warehouses as they dared, then headed off-road to park. With the Beagle safely out of sight behind a clump of trees, the pair of them sneaked over to the parking lots.

Staying close together, ducking behind the vehicles so they wouldn't be seen, they moved down the rows of parked cars and trucks. They checked each one in turn as they went, looking for a maker's insignia or a logo.

Leah soon spotted a big truck, all black with tinted windows and with huge chunky tyres. The tyres had fresh mud on them. The truck had a greenish, rearing snake spray-painted on one of the sides. As the Biology Explorer, she recognised the snake instantly. It was a pit viper! And it was definitely striking...

"This has to be it," she told Gustavo, her heart thumping with excitement. "A truck called a Viper Strike!"

"Then this has to be the poachers' warehouse," Gustavo said. "We're right on top of them!"

The warehouse had double doors standing wide open. There was no way to get through them without being spotted, so Leah and Gustavo sneaked around to the back.

There were no windows on the ground floor, but there were some little ones high up on the wall. Luckily, there was a sturdy-looking tree growing close by. They quickly climbed up among its feathery leaves.

Leah straddled a branch and pulled herself closer and closer to the warehouse, until she could see in through the grimy upper window. She tried not to look down. The ground seemed a long way below them.

"Can you see anything?" Gustavo asked.

"Plenty," Leah whispered. "There are dozens of crates inside, all filled with Venus flytraps!"

Gustavo punched the air and Leah grinned in triumph. At last the hunt was over. The poachers must have thought they'd gotten away with it. But now the Secret Explorers had found them...

Chapter Seven
THE TRAP IS SET

Clinging tightly to her perch up in the tree, Leah watched through the warehouse window. The poachers were hard at work. Four of them were packing the stolen flytraps up into crates. The other two – the man and woman she'd seen the night before – were wheeling the crates out on a trolley and loading them into the cars and trucks.

Leah noticed the window was slightly open. Maybe if she shuffled closer, she'd be able to hear the poachers talking.

She made up her mind and edged further along the branch. It gave a sinister creak... but it held.

"What do you think you're doing?" came the woman's angry voice. "Having a party? These all need to be boxed up by tonight! Do you want to be the one who has to tell my buyer that half their plants are missing?"

"We're working as fast as we can," complained a sweaty poacher. "And it's hot in here!"

The woman grabbed a plant spray bottle and squirted the poacher in the face with it. "There! Better? Now quit your whining and get back to work."

As the miserable poacher hurried to pack more plants, Leah turned to Gustavo in horror. "Did you hear that? They're planning to sell the plants tonight!"

"That doesn't leave us with much time," Gustavo said. "What are we going to do?"

Leah thought hard. Whenever the Secret Explorers went on a mission, the Beagle always made sure they had all the equipment they needed, even if they didn't always know it at first. So what did they have that she could use?

Leah went down the list in her mind. They had the camping gear, which they'd put back inside the Beagle. Food – but they'd eaten that. Then there was the tablet. She'd tried to video the poachers with it, but without any luck. All she'd been able to record with it were some blurry images and bear noises...

Just like that, an idea began to take shape in her mind. She thought of the Venus flytrap closing its spiky leaves shut over the bug. Maybe they needed to set a trap of their own!

"Gustavo, I've got a plan," she said. "It's risky, but it might work! Listen. Here's what we do..."

*

Leah and Gustavo sneaked back to the Beagle. They put a video call through to Luisa at the conservation centre.

"We've found the poachers," Leah said. "Sending you the location now. Can you notify the rangers and get here as quick as you can? They're leaving any moment!"

"Of course," Luisa said. Her eyes were wide with surprise. "But how are you going to keep the poachers there? They could drive off at any minute, and they're not going to sit and wait for us to arrive!"

"Leave it to us," Leah said, and gave her a salute.

Gustavo grabbed the tent ropes from the Beagle's cargo pod, while Leah took the tablet. Together they crept back to the warehouse. While Leah kept a wary eye out for the poachers, Gustavo hid the ropes under a bush.

So far, so good. Now for the tricky part.

They climbed back up the tree. Gustavo kept watch while Leah wriggled along the branch until she reached the window. The poachers were still hard at work inside, scrambling about like bugs. *You'd better watch out for trigger hairs, poachers,* Leah thought.

Time to spring the trap. Leah made sure the tablet's playback volume was at maximum. The Beagle had made it so it was

supercharged – and went a lot louder than most devices could manage. She held it up to the window and pressed "PLAY".

Extraordinary sounds began to blast out of the tablet and echo around the roof. Snorting, growling, snuffling sounds – the sounds of a bear trampling through the undergrowth and hunting for food. But to the poachers inside the building, it must have sounded like nothing on earth.

They stopped working and looked at one another with fearful faces.

"What in the heck is that?" said one of them.

"Busted ventilator?" said another. "Or a bobcat got into the vents?"

Just then, the tablet played a long, rattling growl.

"Boss!" yelled the sweaty poacher. "We've got some kind of situation here!"

The two lead poachers were already running into the warehouse from outside. "What's that noise?" demanded the woman in charge. "Where's it coming from? One of you go and check it out!"

Leah looked back at Gustavo and grinned. He gave her a thumbs-up – the plan was working! The noises had drawn the poachers into the warehouse. *Just like Venus flytraps using nectar to lure insects*, Leah thought. Now all she and Gustavo had to do was shut the jaws of their trap.

She set the tablet to play the bear noises on a loop. Then she and Gustavo quickly climbed down the tree, ran and grabbed the ropes from under the bush, and sprinted round to the front of the warehouse to the open double doors.

The head poacher saw them and her eyes went wide. "Hey! Stop right there, kids!"

Leah ignored her. As the woman came running towards them, Leah and Gustavo grabbed the doors and slammed them shut, like the spiny head of a Venus flytrap snapping closed.

An angry bang came from inside. Panting hard, Leah and Gustavo lashed the rope around the door handles and tied it tightly.

"Got you," Leah gasped. "Like bugs in a flytrap!"

She could hardly believe it. The plan had worked!

But the poachers weren't giving up easily. Shouts and yells came from inside. The doors shivered as the poachers' fists pounded on them.

Leah and Gustavo stepped back, exchanging anxious looks. The doors were metal. They'd hold up to a battering – wouldn't they?

But then there was a heavy crash from inside. And now Leah looked at the door, it was rustier than she'd thought. One of the hinges looked like it was going to give way.

Another crash. Part of the door frame fell off and landed with a rattling clang on the tarmac.

"Uh oh," Gustavo said.

Leah gulped. She'd thought they'd won. But now it looked like her plan to save the Venus flytraps was about to go horribly wrong...

Chapter Eight
FLYTRAP RESCUE

Wham! The warehouse doors buckled outwards as yet another blow landed.

"You're in big trouble, kids!" the woman yelled from inside. The doors were open a crack now. Leah could see the woman's angry face glaring at her. Wham! The ropes strained against the door handles.

Gustavo grabbed Leah's arm and pulled

her further back. She held her breath as she saw dent after dent appear on the doors. They weren't built to withstand this much force, and they were old and battered. Any moment now, they'd give.

If she and Gustavo started running now, they might escape... but the plants would be lost forever. Leah clenched her fists and stood her ground. Gustavo was by her side.

Wham-kerspanggg!

One of the door hinges flew off. The next blow would definitely smash them open.

But then, Leah heard an engine noise drawing closer. A fanfare of happy beeps rang out. It was the conservation centre's all-terrain vehicle, zooming back up the road, with Luisa at the wheel!

"You made it!" Leah cheered. She ran towards the approaching vehicle, just as the warehouse doors crashed to the ground.

The crowd of angry poachers burst out of the building and started rushing towards Leah and Gustavo, but then they froze in fear. They'd heard something. Leah heard it too – the unmistakeable wailing of a police siren. The poachers ran in different directions, but it was no use. Seconds later, three police cars came screeching into the parking lot, their blue lights flashing. The cars had hardly stopped before the officers jumped out and raced after the poachers.

Leah and Gustavo both gave Luisa a hug. "We're so glad to see you!" Leah said.

"That was a wild drive!" said Luisa.

One by one, the police officers brought the poachers back to the cars. The poachers' hands were cuffed. They glared at Leah as they went past, and the woman shook her head furiously. "You bunch of clods!" she yelled at the other poachers. "How could you let these two kids trick you?"

"That's enough out of you," said a police officer. "You're under arrest!" He shut her into the back of his car.

With the poachers out of the way, it was safe to head into the warehouse. Luisa looked around at all the stolen Venus flytraps in their trays and clapped her hands with delight. "I can't believe it! There must be thousands of plants here. You've saved them all!"

"We're just glad we could help," Gustavo said. "But what happens now?"

"My team and I will take care of them at the conservation centre, then return them to the wild when they're strong enough," said Luisa. "In fact, there's a batch of flytraps that are about ready to be replanted now, if the pair of you would like to lend a hand?"

"We'd love to!" Leah and Gustavo said together.

Not long after, the two of them were kneeling on the soft forest ground, digging a series of holes with little trowels. Leah carefully took the first of the healthy flytraps from its cultivation tray, lowered it into the hole and gently slid the soil back in over the roots. "Good luck," she whispered to it.

"I think you've done this kind of thing before," Luisa said approvingly.

"Yes, but not with these plants," said Leah. "I've never had a Venus flytrap of my own."

Luisa smiled. "Is that so?"

Once all the flytraps were safely bedded into their new homes, Luisa called Leah and Gustavo over. "I have a surprise for you. Here. I know you'll look after it."

She handed Leah a flytrap to take home. She said, "This isn't a wild one, of course! I bred it myself. It's easy to do, so there's no need for poachers to steal them from the wild."

"Thank you!" Leah and Gustavo said happily. Leah cradled her plant in her hands.

They said goodbye to Luisa and her team, headed back to the Beagle and strapped themselves in. Leah gave Gustavo a fist-bump.

"Mission accomplished," she said with a happy sigh. The Beagle made an electronic whistle, as if to say: "and thank goodness for that!"

The button that had read "START" now read "HOME". Leah pressed it.

Brilliant light flared up around them. The Beagle rushed forward, picking up speed as if they were heading down a rollercoaster. It rattled and shook as it went. The huge chunky wheels shrank down into little wobbly ones. The big frame dwindled to a little metal frame held together with duct tape and string. In moments it was nothing but a clapped out old go-kart again.

The light faded, and Leah and Gustavo were back in the Exploration Station once more.

All the other Secret Explorers came crowding around. "Brilliant job," said Connor, and they all agreed.

"Yeah, especially the way you used that bear recording!" said Kiki.

Everyone sat together while Leah and Gustavo excitedly talked them through the mission. They passed the flytrap around so they could all get a good look.

Tamiko grinned. "It almost looks like a tiny tyrannosaur mouth!"

"Or an alien," said Roshni.

"From Venus?" Ollie joked.

Kiki took the plant and put it in the botanical display case, where the temperature would be correct and special lamps would give it all the daylight it needed. Leah knew it'd be safe there.

It was time to go. Leah hugged Gustavo, said goodbye to all the others, and stepped back through the glowing door.

For a few giddying seconds, bright light blazed and a strong wind roared around her. Then, as if she had never left, she found herself standing back home outside her greenhouse.

She pushed the door open. Her plants were all thriving. It made her proud to see them so healthy and well looked after.

Luisa did say Venus flytraps were easy to grow, didn't she? Leah thought. *I wonder how easy it is? Well, there's only one way to find out!*

She leaned over her plants, and whispered, "I think you lot are going to get a new friend soon. Let's all make them very welcome, okay? They look a bit strange, and they've got quite an unusual diet..."

MISSION NOTES

THE VENUS FLYTRAP

Most plants need water and sunlight to survive, but for some, that's not enough. Carnivorous plants catch and "eat" insects or other small animals and digest them to gain extra nutrients. The world's most famous carnivorous plant is the Venus flytrap.

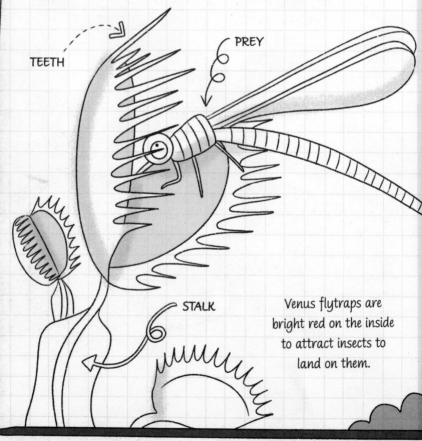

TEETH

PREY

STALK

Venus flytraps are bright red on the inside to attract insects to land on them.

HOW VENUS FLYTRAPS WORK

When an insect lands on a Venus flytrap and comes into contact with tiny "trigger hairs", the plant's hinged leaves snap shut. This creates a cage around the insect. The plant then creates a special substance that digests their prey.

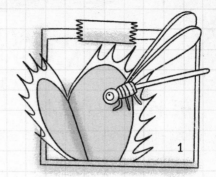

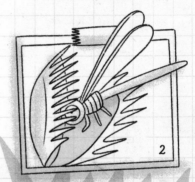

Venus flytraps only clamp shut if two trigger hairs are touched in quick succession. This means the leaves will detect prey, but won't trigger for false alarms such as drops of rain.

OTHER CARNIVOROUS PLANTS

There are more than 500 species of carnivorous plant, and they all have various clever ways of catching and digesting their prey.

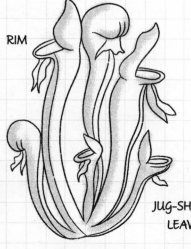

RIM

JUG-SHAPED LEAVES

PITCHER PLANTS ARE QUITE LARGE, SO CAN DIGEST MICE AND FROGS AS WELL AS INSECTS.

SARRACENIAS

Also known as "pitcher plants", sarracenia have slippery jug-shaped leaves with a pool of liquid at the bottom. The plants produce a sweet nectar around the rim, which lures insects to them. When the insects land, they slip and fall into the pool below, where they are slowly digested.

There are more
than 40 kinds
of butterwort.

BUTTERWORTS

The leaves of a butterwort are covered in two
substances, a glue that traps insects that land on
them, and another that helps digest them. Butterworts
are sometimes kept in greenhouses to control pests.

Most carnivorous
plants grow where the
soil doesn't provide
many nutrients.

LONG LEAVES

☰ SUNDEWS

These plants grow in bogs. They are covered with sticky
hairs that have a bead of glue at the end. If an insect
mistakes this glue for a drop of water and lands on the
plant, it becomes stuck. Then, nearby hairs on the plants
fold over the insect and start to digest it.

CAROLINA WILDLIFE

Venus flytraps only grow naturally in the wild in a small area across North and South Carolina, USA. Not only is this area home to many plant species, it's also home to lots of varied wildlife.

BLACK BEAR
* LENGTH: Up to 1.8m (6ft)
* WEIGHT: Up to 300kg (660lb)
* DIET: Grass, fruit, fish

Black bears are known for their size and strength, but they're surprisingly agile. They can run at up to 40kph (25mph) and can climb trees with ease.

ARMADILLO
* LENGTH: Up to 57cm (22in)
* WEIGHT: Up to 6.5kg (14lb)
* DIET: Insects, fruit

Although armadillos are good swimmers, they often walk underwater to cross streams. They can hold their breath for more than 5 minutes!

FLYING SQUIRREL

* LENGTH: Up to 15cm (6in)
* WEIGHT: Up to 140g (0.3lb)
* DIET: Leaves, nuts, fruit

Bats are the only mammals capable of true flight, but these squirrels have a special flap of skin that acts like a parachute and allows them to glide over long distances. They even use their tail to steer!

BOBCAT

* LENGTH: Up to 110cm (43in)
* WEIGHT: Up to 18kg (40lb)
* DIET: Small mammals, birds

Bobcats are solitary animals, and fiercely protect their territory from rivals. Unlike most cats, they have short stubby tails.

GREAT HORNED OWL

* LENGTH: Up to 60cm (23in)
* WEIGHT: Up to 2.5kg (5lb)
* DIET: Small mammals, birds, insects, reptiles

QUIZ

1   What rare flower does Leah find near her home before heading to the Exploration Station?

2   True or false: A botanist is a scientist who studies animals.

3   What name is given to plants that trap and eat animals?

4   True or false: Venus flytraps are the same size as an adult person.

5   What type of bear do the Secret Explorers encounter?

6   True or false: ATV stands for "All-terrain vehicle".

7   What do the Secret Explorers bring back to the Exploration Station?

SEARCH FOR FLIES

There are five flies
to spot in this book.
Can you find them all?

They look
like this!

Check your answers on page 127

GLOSSARY

ATV
An "all-terrain vehicle" that allows a rider to travel across various terrains. Also known as a quad bike

BOTANIST
A scientist who studies plants

CARNIVORE
A plant or animal that eats animals

CHLOROPHYLL
The substance in plants that gives them their green colour and helps them get energy from sunlight

CONSERVATION CENTRE
A place or area dedicated to the protection of wildlife and the environment

EXTINCT

An animal or plant that has died out and no longer exists

FUNGI

A group of living things that break down dead plants and animals to make their food

GPS

A radio navigation system that enables people to determine exact locations on Earth and obtain directions

GREENHOUSE

A glass building that protects plants from cold weather

INSECTIVORES

Animals that eat insects

INSIGNIAS

A badge or emblem, usually associated with an organization

NOCTURNAL

Animals that are active at night

NUTRIENTS
A substance
that gives a living
thing the energy
or chemicals it
needs to survive

POACHERS
People who
illegally catch or
steal wildlife

SEED BANK
A place where
seeds are stored
to preserve them
for the future

SEEDLING
A young plant

VENUS FLYTRAP
A small carnivorous
plant

WAREHOUSE
A large building
used for storage

Quiz answers

1. Ghost orchid

2. False

3. Carnivorous

4. False

5. Black bear

6. True

7. A Venus flytrap

For Erik

Text for DK by Working Partners Ltd
9 Kingsway, London WC2B 6XF
With special thanks to Adrian Bott

Design by Collaborate Ltd
Illustrator Ellie O'Shea
Consultant Anita Ganeri

Acquisitions Editor James Mitchem
Designer Sonny Flynn
Publishing Coordinator Issy Walsh
Senior Production Editor Robert Dunn
Production Controller Francesca Sturiale
Publishing Director Sarah Larter

First published in Great Britain in 2021 by
Dorling Kindersley Limited
One Embassy Gardens, 8 Viaduct Gardens,
London, SW11 7AY

A CIP catalogue record for this book
is available from the British Library.
ISBN: 978-0-2414-4541-9

Printed and bound in Great Britain by
Clays Ltd, Elcograf S.p.A.

For the curious
www.dk.com

The publisher would like to thank Jo Chukualim and Lynne Murray for
picture library assistance, and Caroline Twomey for proofreading.